On the trail of Cosmic Cousin . . .

Eunice kept her fingers crossed every time she checked the table. Two days later, as she slid her hand over the book on the ledge, she thought it felt different from *Aliens I Have Known*. This was a thicker book. She pulled it out to take a peek. It was a book she'd never seen before—*The Return of the Martian Zyvitch*—and there was a note in it:

Dear Solar Soulmate,
 Leaving books under the table is a great idea. You'll like this book. Chapter 7 is fantastic!
 Your Cosmic Cousin

Eunice could hardly believe it! Cosmic Cousin had found her note and had actually written back! Now that this plan had worked, Eunice was sure she could find out Cosmic Cousin's identity.

Other Bantam Skylark Books you will enjoy
Ask your bookseller for the books you have
missed

BE A PERFECT PERSON IN JUST THREE DAYS!
  by Stephen Manes
THE CASTLE IN THE ATTIC
  by Elizabeth Winthrop
THE DINOSAUR TOOTH (Annie K.'s Theater
  #1) by Sharon Dennis Wyeth
ENCYCLOPEDIA BROWN BOY DETECTIVE
  by Donald J. Sobol
FELITA by Nicholosa Mohr
THE GHOST SHOW (Annie K.'s Theater #2)
  by Sharon Dennis Wyeth
HILARY TO THE RESCUE (Pets, Inc. #3)
  by Jennifer Armstrong
I'LL MEET YOU AT THE CUCUMBERS
  by Lilian Moore
THE MAGIC OF MYRA C. WAXWEATHER
  by Sandra Dutton
THE PUPPY PROJECT (Pets, Inc. #1)
  by Jennifer Armstrong
THIRTEEN MEANS MAGIC (Abracadabra #1)
  by Eve Becker
TIME AT THE TOP by Edward Ormondroyd
TOO MANY PETS (Pets, Inc. #2)
  by Jennifer Armstrong

Cosmic Cousin

by Nancy Hayashi

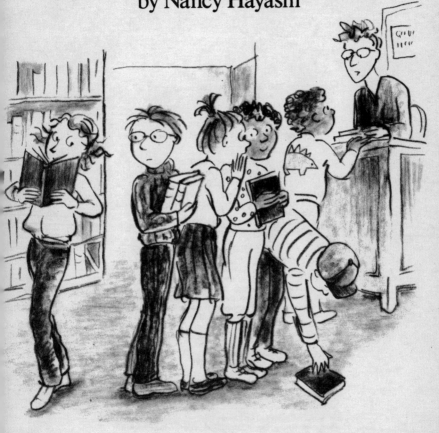

A BANTAM SKYLARK BOOK®
New York • Toronto • London • Sydney • Auckland

RL 3, 007–010
This edition contains the complete text
of the original hardcover edition.
NOT ONE WORD HAS BEEN OMITTED.

COSMIC COUSIN

A Bantam Skylark Book / published by arrangement with
E.P. Dutton

PRINTING HISTORY
E.P. Dutton edition published 1988

Bantam edition / December 1990

Skylark Books is a registered trademark of Bantam Books, a division of Bantam Doubleday Dell Publishing Group, Inc. Registered in U.S. Patent and Trademark Office and elsewhere.

ISBN 0-553-15841-4

Published simultaneously in the United States and Canada

Bantam Books are published by Bantam Books, a division of Bantam Doubleday Dell Publishing Group, Inc. Its trademark, consisting of the words "Bantam Books" and the portrayal of a rooster, is Registered in U.S. Patent and Trademark Office and in other countries. Marca Registrada. Bantam Books, 666 Fifth Avenue, New York, New York 10103.

PRINTED IN THE UNITED STATES OF AMERICA

CWO   0 9 8 7 6 5 4 3 2 1

to Barbara Bottner

Contents

1   Who Can It Be?   1

2   Solar Soulmate   8

3   The Zyvitch Test   16

4   Clues in the Classroom   26

5   Library Research   33

6   List of Suspects   43

7   Cosmos, Oklahoma   51

8   A Last-Ditch Effort   57

9   All Is Discovered   64

10 Cosmic Surprise   72

1

Who Can It Be?

To Whom It May Concern,
If you liked this book, try _Trapped in the Asteroid Belt._ Your Cosmic Cousin

Eunice Butler was sprawled on the bottom bunk, halfway through _Terrors of the Time Warp,_ when she found this message. It was written on the back of a bookmark.

"Alma, listen to this." She read the note out loud to her older sister in the top bunk.

"Who do you think wrote this? Alma? ALMA!"

Alma dragged her eyes away from her own book, *Prom Night Promises*. "Who wrote what?"

Eunice read the note again.

"Let me see that." Alma took the bookmark carefully so she wouldn't smear her nail polish. Their mother allowed them to use nail polish in the eighth grade, and Alma had wasted no time.

"Trapped in the Asteroid Belt." Alma wrinkled her nose. "Sounds like a terrible book. Here."

Eunice grabbed the bookmark back. It sounded like a wonderful book to her. She read the note again and then turned it over. "Hey! Cosmic Cousin must go to my school. This is one of the bookmarks we got on the first day of school. I wonder who it is."

She studied the handwriting. It was sort of a cross between printing and script. She liked the way it looked.

Who could it be? she wondered. It was exciting to find a message from someone who liked the same sort of books she liked. It was even more exciting to think that whoever it was went to her school and might be someone she knew. But who? How could she figure it out? The handwriting was her only clue. She knew she would recognize it if she saw it again.

The next day, Eunice held her breath as she hunted through the shelves for *Trapped in the Asteroid Belt*. She found it at last and sat right down on the library steps to read the first chapter. After the first chapter, she went on to the second. Eunice liked to read so much that once she started she had a hard time stopping. In the summer reading club at the library, she had read more books than anyone in her grade. Her spaceship had zoomed all the way to Pluto on the reading-club chart.

After chapter 5 she began to walk slowly, looking up from the book only when she reached street corners. She was almost at her front door when she found another bookmark and another note.

Eunice raced back to the library. She flipped impatiently through the card catalog for the title and then searched the shelves. *Invasion of the Pluto People* was in. Her luck was holding. As she went to check it out, she wondered if there was a note in this one. That would be perfect. Another note and then another book and then another note . . .

"EUNICE BUTLER! What are you doing to that book? You'll break the spine shaking it like that," said Mrs. Rindfuss, the librarian.

"Sorry, Mrs. Rindfuss."

"And please try to take out *all* your books at one time," Mrs. Rindfuss said, firmly pressing her glasses to her nose.

QUIET
PLEASE

Eunice studied the picture on the cover and read a few pages before putting the new book into her backpack. *Invasion of the Pluto People* looked good but there was no note in it. At least, none had fallen out when she shook it. Had she come to the end of the notes already?

She glanced around the library as she backed out the door. Cosmic Cousin might be here at this very moment, looking like any other kid. Who could it be? Whoever it was, Cosmic Cousin sure had great taste in books.

That night, Eunice had trouble deciding which new book to read. This was the kind of trouble she liked. She could finish *Trapped in the Asteroid Belt* since she only had four more chapters to go. Or she could start *Invasion of the Pluto People*. Finally, she settled on *Invasion of the Pluto People*. If this was Cosmic Cousin's favorite book, she couldn't go wrong.

It *was* good—so good she finished it by flashlight, under the covers, even though it was hard to do because she had to hold the flashlight with her teeth when she turned the pages.

Up to the very end, she hoped to find another message from Cosmic Cousin—perhaps scribbled in the margin—but there was none. Eunice was depressed. At last she fell asleep with her head under the covers.

Solar Soulmate

The next morning, Eunice woke up early. Her head was still under the covers, and her ear was jammed against the flashlight.

She lay in bed, rubbing her sore ear and thinking about the notes from Cosmic Cousin. Finally she got out of bed to find her backpack. The two notes were in there, tucked in the secret compartment of her pencil box. She read the first note. It told her nothing new. Then, as she was reading the second note, she had a great idea. *Invasion of the Pluto People* was Cosmic Cousin's favorite book—good enough to read twice. There was just a chance Cosmic Cousin would read it again. Eunice sometimes did that with books she liked. She decided to write her own note.

Dear Cosmic Cousin,
I really liked this book!
Have you read <u>Aliens I Have Known</u>? It's almost always out, so if I find it for you, I'll put it under the library table by the window.
Your Solar Soulmate
P.S. There's a ledge under the table.

Eunice opened *Invasion of the Pluto People* and wedged her note as tightly as possible into the binding. After school that day, she took it back to the library.

Then she looked for *Aliens I Have Known.* For once, the book was in. She thought this was a good sign her plan would work. Checking to see that no one was watching, she hid the book on the ledge under the table by the window. There. Now all she had to do was wait for Cosmic Cousin to reread the book, find her note, and look under the table.

But Eunice was not very good at waiting. She checked under the table after school every day for a week. *Aliens I Have Known* was still hidden there. She also looked to see if *Invasion of the Pluto People* had been taken out. No luck. It was still on the shelf.

One week went by. When Eunice was at he library, instead of paying attention to her work, she studied the other kids, trying to figure out which one was her mysterious pen pal. It could be anyone. Remembering the bookmark, she kept her eye on the kids from her school. A lot of them took the bus to the library after school and hung around for a while. Some of them did homework or got out books to read—especially when Mrs. Rindfuss was watching—and some of them just talked.

Eunice decided to start first with the kids who came to the library a lot.

Walter Kenney was usually there. He must have sensed Eunice staring at him because he looked up and smiled. Embarrassed, she smiled back and then quickly looked the other way.

Rachel Poindexter and Janie Hines were at the next table, talking and giggling. Rachel was talking, as usual, and Janie was giggling. The new kid, Mary Louise Butterman, was studying quietly beside them.

Then there was Eddie Mumford, reading and chewing gum. The faster he read, the faster his jaws moved. Eunice watched Eddie and wondered what he was reading.

Stanley Ferguson was sitting across from Eddie. Eunice didn't have to wonder what he was reading. It *had* to be a book about dinosaurs. He was wearing his sweatshirt with the stegosaurus on the back.

Later, on her way to the drinking fountain, she saw her neighbor, Marcie Hubble, checking out books. She was with Joey Gebhart. Joey didn't have many books but they were very thick. They looked interesting. But Eunice couldn't get close enough to read the titles.

By the beginning of the next week, Eunice was getting desperate. Maybe Cosmic Cousin would *never* find her note.

Then she discovered *Invasion of the Pluto People* wasn't on the shelf anymore. Cosmic Cousin could have taken it out to reread it.

Eunice kept her fingers crossed every time she checked the table. Two days later, as she slid her hand over the book on the ledge, she thought it felt different from *Aliens I Have Known*. This was a thicker book. She pulled it out to take a peek. It was a book she'd never seen before—*The Return of the Martian Zyvitch*—and there was a note in it:

Dear Solar Soulmate,
    Leaving books under the table is a great idea. You'll like this book. Chapter 7 is fantastic!   Your Cosmic Cousin

---

Eunice could hardly believe it! Cosmic Cousin had found her note and had actually written back! Now that this plan had worked,

Eunice was sure she could find out Cosmic Cousin's identity. It would be exciting to follow clues and figure it out for herself. Someday soon she'd be able to say "Hello, Cosmic Cousin" and watch the look of surprise as they greeted each other.

Holding her new book tightly, Eunice went to look for *Orbiting the Planet of Doom*. That was the next book she wanted to leave for Cosmic Cousin. Her heart was singing as she tucked it onto the ledge under the table.

3

The Zyvitch Test

Her best friend, Arnold Cosgrove, came by while Eunice was sitting on her front steps reading *The Return of the Martian Zyvitch*. Arnold lived three houses down the street and was in her class at school. In fact, he sat next to her. Today he was looking even happier than usual.

"Have you read these yet?" He handed Eunice two *Unknown Galaxy* comic books.

"Hey, thanks, Arnold! I've never read these. Where did you get them?"

"I traded five of my old *Curse of the Vampire* comic books for them," Arnold said, wiggling his ears. He had just discovered he could do this, and he liked to keep in practice.

Eunice was pleased. *Unknown Galaxy* comic books were her favorites, and she knew Arnold had gotten them just for her. Any other time she would have started in on them immediately, but right now she was anxious to get on to chapter 7 in *Return of the Martian Zyvitch*.

"You should read this, Arnold." Eunice showed him the cover of her book. He didn't seem interested.

"Oh, I don't know. It looks like a long book," Arnold said. He had a pencil tucked above one ear and was trying to wiggle it loose.

"It's not that long. Just listen to the plot. There's a Zyvitch—that's a sort of space witch—and she rides around in a black hole trying to syphon sunshine from all the planets." Eunice gave him a summary as far as chapter 6. "It would make a great comic book," she added.

Now Arnold looked interested. He liked to read comic books, but he liked to make up his own even more. Arnold was the best artist in the class. It was fun to sit next to him, watching him work on his comic books and reading the funny notes he gave her when their teacher wasn't looking.

"Is that the book you're giving your oral report on tomorrow?" Arnold asked.

"No. I'm giving mine on *Terrors of the Time Warp*. This is a book someone sort of gave me."

"Who gave it to you?" Arnold asked. "It looks like a library book to me."

Eunice hesitated. Should she tell Arnold about Cosmic Cousin? It would be fun to tell. And maybe Arnold could help her figure out who it was. On the other hand . . .

"Hi. What are you two talking about? Is it a secret?"

Eunice looked around quickly. She saw Marcie Hubble from next door. Marcie was in her class, too.

"Oh, nothing much," Eunice said. She was glad she hadn't been telling Arnold about Cosmic Cousin. Now she realized she wanted to keep it to herself. She especially didn't want Marcie to find out about it. Marcie *loved* secrets. And she could make one out of anything. Her birthday had been a month ago but she still hadn't told Eunice what her best present was. That was a secret. She wouldn't even tell Eunice her middle name. That was a secret, too. But if Marcie thought Eunice had a secret, she'd keep after her to tell. So

Eunice was relieved when Marcie started talking about Halloween.

"What are you guys going to be?" Marcie asked. "It's only two weeks away, you know. I can't decide whether to be a butterfly or a bag of jelly beans."

"You're crazy!" Arnold laughed. "How can you be a bag of jelly beans?"

"It's easy. You get one of those big, clear plastic bags, and you stuff it with little balloons. Then you step into it and tie it around your neck. And you put a label on the front— YUMMY JELLY BEANS. What are you guys going to be?" Marcie asked again.

"I'm going to be a vampire bat," Arnold said. He explained how he was going to attach the bat ears to his own and wiggle them. "But I have to build up my ear muscles first," he admitted.

"I want to be a UFO but I don't know how to make the costume," Eunice said.

Marcie sighed. "I wanted to be a ladybug but that new kid is going to be one. She told

me she already has the costume from last year."

"You mean Mary Louise? So let old Cheesy Lou-weesy be a ladybug and you can be a bug lady. Or a buggy lady." Arnold started jumping around, slapping imaginary bugs off his arms and legs.

"That's not funny, Arnold." Marcie glared at him. "And stop calling her Cheesy Lou-weesy."

"Oh, you always stick up for the under-dog," Eunice said. "Nobody likes her."

"Well, I think she's nice. By the way," Marcie said, changing the subject, "I saw you at the library, Eunice, but you didn't see me." Marcie smiled as if she knew a secret and wouldn't tell. "I was just returning my book-report book."

All at once Eunice was curious. She had known Marcie since kindergarten but she didn't know what kind of books Marcie liked to read. "What's the name of your book?" she asked.

"You'll find out tomorrow when I give my book report." Marcie smiled again.

"Well, I'm not all *that* interested, you know," Eunice said.

But she was. She wondered why Marcie had mentioned seeing her at the library. Could

Marcie have noticed her reaching under the table for the book from Cosmic Cousin?

Could *Marcie* be Cosmic Cousin?

Eunice hadn't thought of it before, but it was possible. After all, Marcie did go to her school, and Eunice did see her at the library sometimes.

Eunice quickly decided on a way to check out this new possibility. "I've changed my mind about Halloween," she said. "I think I'll go as a Martian Zyvitch."

"Hey, that sounds good," Arnold said.

"What's a Zyvitch?" Marcie asked.

Was she just pretending she didn't know? Eunice watched Marcie carefully as she explained what a Zyvitch was, but she couldn't tell a thing from the look on Marcie's face. Knowing Marcie, even if she were Cosmic Cousin, she'd never give up her secret so easily.

"It's time for dinner," Eunice's mother called.

"See you guys tomorrow," Eunice said. And maybe that's not all I'll see, she thought. The book reports might give her some more clues about Cosmic Cousin.

Clues in the Classroom

"Eunice Butler, please write your book title on the board," said Mrs. Gillies.

As usual, Eunice was the first to give her book report. Mrs. Gillies liked to do everything in an orderly, alphabetical way. Eunice wished a few *A* names would join the class so she wouldn't have to be first all year.

While Eunice told the class about *Terrors of the Time Warp*, she looked around to see if anyone was especially interested. Everyone was interested, but it was an exciting book. When she got to the part about the space captain suddenly shrinking to the size of an atom, all eyes were on her. But she couldn't tell if two of those eyes were Cosmic Cousin's.

Mrs. Gillies called on Mary Louise Butterman next. Mary Louise was Eunice's study buddy. And all because of their last names. *B* for Butler. *B* for Butterman. *B* for boring. Eunice wished she weren't stuck with Mary Louise. Study buddies were important. You got to study together for the last fifteen minutes every day, and sometimes longer before a big test. Almost *anyone* would be more fun to study with than Mary Louise. She seemed so quiet, it was hard to get a hello out of her. Why, if she hadn't moved to their school, Arnold would be Eunice's study buddy. Butler and Cosgrove—now that would be fun.

"Speak up, Mary Louise. I can't hear you," Mrs. Gillies said.

"My report isn't finished yet," Mary Louise said, a little louder.

Mrs. Gillies sighed. "Well then, we'll have to go on to Arnold."

Arnold's book report was very short, but he stretched it out by drawing the characters' faces on the board. He even wiggled his ears once.

The book reports went on. Eunice paid close attention to all of them, looking for clues. But nothing was turning up. Stanley Ferguson had read a book on dinosaurs, naturally. Joey Gebhart had read a long book on the discovery of rubber and gave a long report.

Eunice's spine was beginning to *feel* like rubber, and she was getting too sleepy to concentrate. She glanced over to see if Arnold was working on his new comic book, "Mrs. Sillies and the Monster Class." He was. With his book-report folder propped up in front as a cover, he was drawing Mrs. Sillies, who looked a lot like the bride of Frankenstein and a little like Mrs. Gillies. Eunice also

recognized some of the monsters he was drawing. They looked like kids in the class.

Then Marcie went to the chalkboard to write her book title. Eunice straightened up to get a good view of the board. Marcie wrote *A Home for Al*. That didn't sound like a good science-fiction title to Eunice.

"Can anyone guess who Al is?" Marcie asked.

Eunice raised her hand. "Is Al short for Alien?" she asked, without much hope.

Some of the kids laughed.

"No, it's not," Marcie said. "Are there any more guesses? Well, Al is just the cutest little black and white alley cat." She showed everyone his picture in the book.

Eunice felt let down. Now she remembered Marcie was a pushover for animals, especially strays. But Marcie might still be Cosmic Cousin, even though her book report didn't prove it. Eunice could just imagine Marcie secretly slipping a note into a book.

Mrs. Gillies called on Eddie Mumford next. As he was writing his title on the board, Eunice snapped to attention. There was something familiar about Eddie's handwriting. It looked like a cross between printing and script. It looked just like the handwriting on the bookmark notes.

"This book is about one of my favorite sports. . . ." Eddie mumbled.

Mrs. Gillies stopped him right there. "Please get rid of your gum, Eddie, and start over."

Eunice was staring so hard at his handwriting that she almost forgot to listen to his re-

port. When she finally tuned in to it, Eddie was saying that the American Indians were the first to play something or other—Eunice wasn't sure what.

"Thank you, Eddie," Mrs. Gillies said when he was done. "I'm sure we all know more about lacrosse now than we did before. The rest of you will give your reports tomorrow."

Well, if Eddie were Cosmic Cousin, you sure couldn't tell it from his book report, Eunice thought. Of course she *could* just ask him straight out—but that would be too easy. She wanted to be able to say, "Ah ha! So *you're* Cosmic Cousin."

Eunice decided to get a closer look at the books Eddie liked to read at the library.

Library Research

After school, Eunice took the bus to the library. She turned in a few books at the desk.

"Only three books, Eunice? You must have a dozen more at home." Mrs. Rindfuss looked at Eunice as if she had better produce those books instantly.

"But they're not due yet," Eunice said. Mrs. Rindfuss sniffed and turned abruptly to the next person in line.

Eunice was smiling as she walked away. It felt so good to have the last word. She looked around for Eddie Mumford. He was there, chewing gum as hard as ever. She decided to stop at the drinking fountain near his table. As she paused behind his chair, she could see he wasn't doing his homework.

"Hi, Eddie. What are you reading?" Eunice asked.

Eddie snapped his gum at her in a friendly way and showed her the front of his book— *Dodge Ball Danny*. Issues of *Sports Illustrated* magazine were piled beside him.

Eunice had to admit Eddie was looking less and less like a candidate for Cosmic Cousin. But as she was thinking this, she glanced at his spelling book. His name was written on the cover in what looked exactly like Cosmic Cousin's handwriting. She couldn't take him off the list yet.

She went to the table by the window, sat down, and checked the ledge under it for a new book. As she did, she looked to see if Eddie was watching. If he really were Cosmic Cousin, he would be interested in that table. There was no new book, and Eddie didn't

seem to be paying attention to her or the table.

She tried to think about what she was reading, but her mind kept racing back to Cosmic Cousin's notes and Eddie's handwriting.

"I can see you've been turning down the pages of these books again."

Eunice looked up to see who Mrs. Rindfuss was scolding.

"I've warned you about this before, Janie," Mrs. Rindfuss said. "Now, I'm sure Rachel *always* uses a bookmark," she continued as she checked in Rachel's books.

Bookmarks again. Eunice gave up trying to remember her math assignment and started to think about Rachel. So Rachel used bookmarks. She was one grade ahead of Eunice but they'd always been friends. Rachel loved to talk and Eunice loved to listen.

The more she thought, the more she liked the idea of Rachel as Cosmic Cousin. She was the one who had gotten Eunice interested in outer space in the first place. Last year, Rachel had wanted to become an astronaut. She had told Eunice all sorts of amazing facts about the universe. The rings of Saturn were actually particles of ice, Rachel had said. Eunice liked to think about them whirling around out there in space.

This year, Rachel wanted to be a veterinarian and told Eunice amazing facts about animals instead. That's how Eunice found out that dogs sweat through their feet and that only female mosquitoes bite.

There was an empty seat across from Eunice. Maybe Rachel would sit there. Eunice wanted to talk to her and also take a look at her handwriting. She could see Rachel heading toward her table. Good. Just then, Mary Louise sat down in the empty seat. Rotten luck, Eunice thought, but she said hello.

"Do you know what pages we were supposed to do for math?" Eunice asked.

"Pages 42 to 60, I think," Mary Louise answered.

"Hey, Mary Louise," Eunice leaned across and whispered. "Did you see what Eddie did with his gum when Mrs. Gillies told him to get rid of it? She thought he threw it in the wastebasket but I saw him put it behind his ear." Eunice laughed. "I'll bet it's still there."

She thought she saw a tiny smile, but Mary Louise didn't look up. Oh, well, you just couldn't get anywhere with some people, Eunice thought as she flipped through her work-book to page 42.

With Cosmic Cousin on her mind, Eunice just couldn't sit still. She decided to get another drink before she started her homework. If she took the long way around to the drinking fountain, past Rachel's table, she might be able to get a glimpse of Rachel's handwriting.

Rachel was talking and laughing with Janie Hines but when she saw Eunice, she motioned to her. "Did you watch that TV show on insects last night?" Rachel whispered.

"No. Was it good?" Eunice whispered back.

"It was great!" Rachel went on. She forgot to whisper now. "The part about earwigs was really *amazing*. You wouldn't believe what a good mother an earwig is. Sit down and I'll tell you how they feed their babies. . . ." Rachel paused to take a breath.

"Tell me tomorrow," Eunice whispered hastily. "I'll meet you at recess." It was hard to stop Rachel once she started talking, and

Eunice could see Mrs. Rindfuss frowning at them. She thought she had better move on. Before she left, she tried to get a look at Rachel's handwriting. But *The Big Book of Penguins* was covering her notebook.

Now it seemed to be animals, animals, and more animals with Rachel. Still, Eunice didn't think Rachel could have completely lost interest in outer space. How could anyone forget those ice rings of Saturn?

Eunice decided to check out one more person before she sat down again. She looked around. Who would be next?

Walter Kenney was a possibility. He came to the library as often as she did, and he always took out lots of books. He went to her school—in fact, he was the friendliest boy there. Thinking about Walter, Eunice began to get her hopes up.

She walked behind his chair and looked quickly to see what he was reading. At least she meant to do it quickly, but she couldn't stop reading.

"Jo! Jo! Where are you?" cried Meg, at the foot of the garret stairs.

"Here!" answered a husky voice from above. . . .

The names seemed very familiar. Eunice realized she was reading *Little Women*. That meant Walter was reading *Little Women*.

Walter looked up at her. He didn't have his usual friendly grin. He seemed embarrassed.

"I was just sort of looking through this book. My sister asked me to get it out for her."

"Hey, it's a good book. Anybody would like it," Eunice said.

Walter glared at her. That hadn't been the right thing to say.

She tried again. "I mean, your sister will really like it." Walter still wasn't smiling.

Eunice slunk back to her table. Well, Walter *had* been the friendliest boy in her school. Now he was going to think she was spying on him. This research business wasn't going very well. Maybe tomorrow there would be some good clues in the rest of the book reports.

Suddenly, she sneezed three times, very loud. Mrs. Rindfuss, shelving books nearby, said, "Eunice Butler, *where* is your handkerchief?"

List of Suspects

The next day, Eunice stayed home with the flu.

"Keep away from my diary, Eunice," Alma warned her as she left to catch the bus. "You can read my new book, though, if you want to."

"*The Summer of Jennifer's Dreams*? I'd rather read the Yellow Pages!" Eunice yelled after her.

Eunice's mother came in to check her temperature. "If you feel too sick to read, you can lie on the couch and watch TV," she said.

"No thanks, Mom, but I'd like a deck of cards and some ginger ale, please."

All morning she played solitaire, sipped ginger ale, and thought about Cosmic Cousin. She didn't want to be sick at home. There she couldn't pick up any more clues about Cosmic Cousin's identity.

Eunice decided to write down a list of kids who might be Cosmic Cousin. After some thought she narrowed it down to five names.

Rachel was first on the list because Eunice thought that deep down Rachel must still have an interest in outer space. After all, someday there would be animals on space colonies. There'd be plenty of work for a veterinarian out there.

Then again, it might be Eddie Mumford. He did *write* like Cosmic Cousin. Maybe he read sports books during the week and science fiction on the weekend.

Walter Kenney was next. She still liked that idea, although she had nothing to go on. Regretfully, she crossed off his name.

Rachel Poindexter
Eddie Mumford
~~Walter Kenney~~
Marcie Hubble
Joey Gebhart

She also put Marcie's name on her list, just because leaving secret notes in books was something Marcie would love to do.

Joey Gebhart was another possibility she'd had in the back of her mind. At the science fair last year, he had won first prize for their level with his Morse code transmitter. Her imagination leaped ahead. Maybe this year they could work on a science-fair project together.

She crawled out of bed to get a Kleenex and to look for her book with the build-it-your-self-telescope plans. She could send away for the lenses if Joey would help pay for them. She moved Joey's name to the top of her list.

That was Wednesday.

By Thursday, Eunice decided Rachel was a better possibility than anyone else. She remembered all those wonderful things that Rachel had told her last year about space.

Friday morning, she favored Eddie over the rest. After all, handwriting never lies. She had read that somewhere.

Friday afternoon, Joey was back in the lead. She had her heart set on the telescope project.

Friday evening, Marcie brought Eunice her homework.

"I have some bad news for you," Marcie said.

"What is it?" Eunice asked uneasily.

"Mrs. Gillies changed Arnold's seat. Now he's up at the front so Mrs. Gillies can keep an eye on him. That's what she said."

"Oh no! What happened? Did she find the comic book he was working on?" Eunice asked.

"Yep. That's what happened. She found 'Mrs. Sillies and the Monster Class.' Arnold can really draw, can't he. Even Mrs. Gillies admitted that," Marcie said.

Eunice sighed. She was going to miss watching Arnold at work.

"Who sits next to me now?" Eunice asked.

"Stanley."

"Oh no. Not Stegosaurus Stanley." Eunice sighed again. All she'd get to watch now would be dinosaur doodles.

Then, cheering up, she thought of a quick test to try on Marcie. Marcie was still on her Cosmic Cousin list—even though she was at the bottom.

"Marcie," Eunice began, "why don't you dress up as a spy for Halloween?" Marcie looked surprised but interested.

"You could dress in black and wear a false beard. . . ." Marcie was looking doubtful now.

"Don't you think it would be fun to be a spy and sneak around leaving secret messages in all sorts of places—like books?" This was daring. She watched Marcie carefully.

"I don't think I'd like a beard," Marcie said. "I'd much rather be a ladybug. By the way, Eunice, may I borrow your red tights for my costume?"

"Sure, but I thought you said Mary Louise was going to be a dumb old ladybug," Eunice said, feeling cross, even though she hadn't really wanted Marcie to be Cosmic Cousin.

"I was wrong about that. I think she's going to be a fairy princess. I saw part of her costume and it's very pretty. All sparkly." Marcie had been rummaging through Eunice's dresser drawer while she talked. Now she held

up the red tights and made a face when she
saw the hole in the toe of the left foot.
"Thanks for the tights," Marcie said as she
left.

Eunice pulled out her list and firmly crossed
off Marcie's name.

Cosmos, Oklahoma

By the time Eunice went back to school, she had worked out a new plan to discover Cosmic Cousin's identity. She got the idea from *Intergalactic Mutiny* and the way Captain Robodek figured out who the real alien was.

She managed to get behind Joey Gebhart in the lunch line, and soon they were talking about the science fair. He wouldn't say much about his project, just hinted that it was pretty advanced.

"My cousin does a lot of interesting experiments like that," Eunice said, putting her plan into operation. "Too bad he doesn't live

around here. He lives in *Cosmos*, Oklahoma."

Joey looked a little bored.

"I call him my *Cosmic Cousin*," Eunice
added hopefully.

Joey moved ahead to pick up his tunabur-
ger.

Oh well, there went the build-it-yourself-
telescope project.

After lunch, Eunice daydreamed through
social studies. She missed having Arnold in the

seat next to her and wondered if he was working on a new comic book. Probably not. Mrs. Gillies was still keeping a very close eye on him.

Toward the end of the day, Eunice was ready for another try at uncovering Cosmic Cousin. After the bell rang, she saw Rachel walking out to wait for the school bus. Eunice grabbed her backpack and ran down the hall after her.

"Where have you been lately?" Rachel asked when she saw Eunice.

"I was sick last week," Eunice answered and then, to start a conversation, she said, "You were going to tell me about the mother earwigs—remember?"

While Rachel talked, Eunice tried to figure out how to work in her Cosmos, Oklahoma, question.

"Animals are really amazing, aren't they?" Rachel said when she had finished. "I'm glad I've decided to be a veterinarian."

Now was her chance. "That reminds me—

I have a cousin who's going to veterinary school," Eunice said.

Rachel looked interested.

"She lives in *Cosmos,* Oklahoma." Rachel looked positively excited now. Eunice's hopes soared. "I call her my Cosmic Cousin." Rachel was about to say something. Just then the bus came.

"I'll save you a seat," Eunice called back to Rachel as she got on the bus. She was glowing inside. Her plan had worked. She had discovered who Cosmic Cousin was! Captain Robodek himself couldn't have done better. As soon as the kids on the bus quieted down, she could talk to Cosmic Cousin at last.

Eunice was just ready to reveal that she was Solar Soulmate when Rachel asked her, "What did you say you call your cousin? How soon is she coming to visit you?"

"What . . . ? Oh, I don't know." Eunice's hopes plunged back to the ground.

"I've got all sorts of questions to ask her," Rachel went on. "Where does she go to

school? In Oklahoma? That's not too far from here. You could ask her to come to see you sometime."

Eunice was too depressed to answer. Finally Rachel lost interest and moved on to other subjects.

"Did I tell you I pulled one of my goldfish through tail rot?" Rachel asked. "I had to sit up all night, nearly, and change the water every fifteen minutes. I think that's what saved him." Rachel paused thoughtfully. "But the other three died."

Rachel talked on but it was hard for Eunice to pay attention. She wished the bus would get to the library soon.

In her mind, she went over her list again. She knew now that it wasn't Rachel or Joey. She had crossed Marcie off her list, and it probably wasn't Eddie. Who did that leave?

Only everybody else at the library!

A Last-Ditch Effort

When the bus reached the library, Rachel and Eunice got off. Because Eunice had been sick, her books were overdue. As she was checking them in and adding up the fines, Mrs. Rindfuss seemed pleased.

"That will be seventy-five cents. I thought you were taking out too many books. What's this I find in your book, Eunice Butler? A *used* Kleenex?"

"No, Mrs. Rindfuss. It's clean." Eunice snatched it back.

Before beginning her homework, Eunice

browsed through the shelves looking for more books to take out. She also looked for *Intergalactic Mutiny* and found it. This was the next book she wanted to leave for Cosmic Cousin. Then she started for the table by the window.

She hurried when she saw someone heading toward her usual seat. Since she hadn't been to the library in nearly a week, someone else might have gotten in the habit of sitting there.

Eunice reached the table first and sat down with relief. Now there should be a book waiting for her. She checked the ledge cautiously with her hand. She could feel a book, but it might be the one she had left for Cosmic Cousin a week ago. Making sure no one was watching, she pulled out the book. Oh, good! It was one she had never read—*The Milky Way and Beyond*. There was a note in it.

Dear Solar Soulmate,
    I just finished this book. The first part is a little boring but keep going— the ending is great! Your Cosmic Cousin

---

Eunice felt a little disappointed. She had sort of been hoping that the next note would be signed with a real name. At first it had been fun to track down clues, but now she just wanted to meet Cosmic Cousin. She wanted to talk to Cosmic Cousin.

Eunice thought of all the things they could do together.

They could camp out in the backyard and make a map of the constellations. Eunice had started one, but it would be more fun to do with somebody.

They could play Eunice's new *Andromeda Galactic Maze* game.

And maybe Cosmic Cousin would help her finish her UFO costume for Halloween.

Eunice thought about how to find out Cosmic Cousin's name. Maybe she should give in and just ask in her next note. It would be so much easier. . . . She thought about it some more.

But no, it wouldn't be as exciting as figuring it out for herself. She would just have to come up with some way to find out who it was.

Before starting to make a new plan, Eunice wrote a note to put into *Intergalactic Mutiny*.

Dear Cosmic Cousin,
    You're going to love this book. And I'll bet you'll never guess who the real alien is.
                    Your Solar Soulmate
P.S. Captain Robodek is my all-time favorite character.

She slipped the book under the table and then concentrated on making her plan. She went over several possibilities before she settled on one. This plan had a couple of drawbacks. She would have to tell a lie, and that bothered Eunice. She decided to think of it as a cover story—like the ones spies and detectives use. The other drawback was whom she had to tell this lie to. Mrs. Rindfuss. There was no getting around that one.

Eunice took some money out of her backpack and went to the desk. She could feel her knees shaking.

"Mrs. Rindfuss."

"Just *one* moment. Can't you see that I'm busy?"

Eunice waited. She felt more nervous than ever.

Finally, Mrs. Rindfuss eyed Eunice over the top of her glasses. "Now what is it you want?"

"I just found a dollar bill in this book." Eunice held up the new book from Cosmic Cousin. "Someone must have used it as a bookmark."

"That was very careless of someone, wasn't it?" Mrs. Rindfuss said.

"I thought maybe you could look up the person who took this book out last. Then you could tell me who it was and I—"

Mrs. Rindfuss cut in. "I simply do not have the time right now to look up something like that."

Eunice turned away, putting the dollar in her pocket. With anyone else but old Rindfuss this plan would have worked.

"However—"

Eunice turned around quickly.

"—you may leave the dollar with me and later I will look up the rightful owner." Mrs. Rindfuss stretched out her hand.

Oh no! Eunice thought fast. "Nooo. I guess I'll just keep it until someone asks you for it."

"Very well, Eunice. As you wish."

Whew! That was close. She had nearly lost her lunch money for the next day.

Now that this plan had failed, Eunice felt she had come to the end of the line.

All Is Discovered

Eunice pushed the dollar farther into her pocket as she walked back to the table by the window. She didn't look up until she was there. Then she saw that Gary Willets was sitting in her seat. He hadn't paid any attention to Eunice's books or her backpack hanging on the chair. She picked up her books and unhooked her backpack. Gary looked up but didn't offer to move. It was a good thing she had already found the new book from Cosmic Cousin and left one in its place.

She sat down at the next table. The library was more crowded and noisy than usual. Some of the sixth graders were really cutting up, drumming their pencils on the tables and throwing erasers.

Mrs. Rindfuss rapped on her desk several times and then came over to their tables. "Stop this racket immediately or you will all have to leave." She glared around at everyone and went back to her desk.

Things were quieter for a few minutes and then one of the sixth graders threw a paper airplane at Gary. It bounced off his head and landed on the floor beside his chair. Eunice felt uneasy as she watched Gary bend over to pick it up. She suddenly wondered if she had shoved the book as far back as usual on the ledge.

"What's this?" she heard him say. Then he shouted, "Hey! Look what I found!"

As he straightened up, she saw he was holding *Intergalactic Mutiny*. He was waving it around. Eunice was frantic that her note might fall out.

"Gary Willets, if you persist in this behavior, I shall have to ask you to leave," Mrs. Rindfuss said.

Just her luck. Any other day, Gary wouldn't have made such a big fuss. Any other day, Mrs. Rindfuss wouldn't have been at his side like a shot.

"I was just saying that I found this book under the table," Gary mumbled. "On a ledge down here—see?"

Mrs. Rindfuss stooped down to examine the ledge. She ran her finger over the book as if to check for dust.

"The very idea of *hiding* books at a public library. Now who would do a thing like that?" She narrowed her eyes at Gary.

"I didn't do it," Gary protested. Suddenly he pointed at Eunice and said, "Why don't you ask her? She was sitting here before."

It was very quiet now. Eunice's heart had nearly stopped when Gary found the book, but now she thought everyone could hear it thudding. She wished *she* could crawl onto a ledge under the table.

"The rest of you boys and girls get back to work." Mrs. Rindfuss came over to Eunice and in a lower voice asked, "Eunice Butler, do you know anything about this?"

"I wasn't sitting there very long," Eunice said, which was the truth—if not the whole truth.

Mrs. Rindfuss looked suspiciously at Eunice. Did she know Eunice was lying—or nearly lying? Then she looked again at the book in her hand and said with surprise, "Why, someone was asking for this very book just the other day."

Mrs. Rindfuss raised her voice again. "I intend to find out who did this." She swept the room with an angry look and marched away.

Oh, if only Mrs. Rindfuss wouldn't find her note in the book, Eunice thought. If only it could fall out now without her seeing it. No chance of that—she had the book in an iron grip.

"You're under arrest, Book," Gary said in

a loud whisper when she had gone. Everyone laughed but Eunice.

Oh, *you* can joke, she thought miserably as she tried to keep her mind on her homework. But every time she thought about what had happened, she broke her pencil.

What would Mrs. Rindfuss do if she found the note? Would she be mad? Eunice tried to remember what she had written in it. Just something about Captain Robodek, she thought. She hadn't signed her name, so no one could know for sure who it was.

Another thought occurred to her. Suppose Mrs. Rindfuss read the note *out loud* to *everyone*? She broke her pencil again.

But the worst part was that she and Cosmic Cousin could never leave books under the table again. How was she going to discover who Cosmic Cousin was? Eunice's spirits sank lower and lower.

It was almost time to leave. Eunice decided to make one last attempt. She was taking a big risk, but she had to get in touch with Cosmic Cousin. She'd leave one more note under the table and hope Mrs. Rindfuss didn't find it. And just in case Cosmic Cousin hadn't been there when the ledge was discovered, she would leave a warning that their hiding place wasn't safe anymore.

Dear Cosmic Cousin,
  We can't leave books here anymore since you-know-who is onto it. Please let me know who you are. I can't tell you my name in case you-know-who finds this note. Wear something red on Thursday when you come to the library, and I'll do the same.
                    Your Solar Soulmate

Eunice hesitated a long time over the "something red" idea, but she couldn't think of anything better. Thursday was two days off. That should give Cosmic Cousin time to find the note. But if Mrs. Rindfuss found it first, she'd be sure to spot Eunice in her red wind-breaker. (Or rather, in Alma's red wind-breaker that Eunice was planning to borrow.) She would have to take that chance.

Eunice waited till almost everyone had gone home. Then she left the note, folded up small, on the ledge under the table.

Cosmic Surprise

It was Thursday, after school, and Eunice was standing just inside the door of the library, watching the kids coming in. All day she had spotted kids in red—red shirts, red sweaters, red backpacks. Now where were they?

Maybe Cosmic Cousin would put on something red at the last minute. Eunice wished she had thought of doing that instead of borrowing Alma's hot, bulky windbreaker. She could have kept her red spaceship pin in her pocket and put it on now.

Checking for something small, she looked

at hair ribbons, belts, shoes, socks. . . . Hey! Walter Kenney was wearing red socks. She never should have crossed Walter off her list.

Eunice walked quickly over to Walter's table. There was no place to sit down so she stood next to his chair.

"Hi, Walter." She zipped the zipper of her windbreaker up and down very fast. Although Walter looked up and gave her a big smile, it wasn't a so-you're-Solar-Soulmate

smile. Eunice stood there for a few more moments, zipping more slowly and feeling silly. Walter didn't look up again but everyone at his table did.

"Sorry, no seats left. Why don't you *zip* on over to another table?" Eddie said. He was still laughing at his own joke as Eunice hurried away. Her face was as red as her jacket.

She sat down at the table by the window and took out her books. She'd be more careful the next time, she thought, and not fall for a stupid little patch of red like that. She tried to think about homework.

Suddenly she caught a flash of red out of the corner of her eye. Janie Hines had just walked in with a red scarf around her neck.

Janie Hines? Why hadn't she thought of her before? After all, Janie was a good friend of Rachel's. And Rachel was the one who had gotten Eunice interested in outer space. Maybe Janie had picked up the same interest from Rachel.

Janie was just the sort of person Eunice

wanted Cosmic Cousin to be. She was fun to talk to. She had a great sense of humor. And she lived only two blocks away from her. Eunice was getting more excited by the minute. She stood up to get Janie's attention.

Then Janie took off the scarf and stuffed it into her pocket. Cosmic Cousin wouldn't do that. Eunice pretended she had needed to stretch and then sat down again. She felt completely let down now. Janie would have been a perfect Cosmic Cousin.

Looking around, she couldn't see any more red, and she began to have dark thoughts. Maybe Cosmic Cousin had never found her note. She checked the table ledge. The note was gone, but what did that mean? Since nobody was wearing red, it must mean Mrs. Rindfuss had found the note. She would have noticed Eunice in the red windbreaker. When she checked out books, Mrs. Rindfuss would point a long bony finger at her and say, "I always knew you were a troublemaker, Eunice Butler."

Eunice decided not to check out any books that day.

Without Cosmic Cousin to look forward to, time passed as slowly as at school. No one new came into the library. The only excitement was when Stanley knocked over the Halloween book display. Marcie and Mary Louise helped him pick up the books. Mrs. Rindfuss blamed all three of them, so Eunice was glad she hadn't helped.

It was almost closing time now, and nearly everyone had gone but Eunice. She was afraid to go by the desk.

Mrs. Rindfuss walked over to Eunice's table and cleared her throat loudly. Here it comes, thought Eunice.

"You had better hurry if you have any books to check out," Mrs. Rindfuss said. "Both of you must have big stacks, as usual. Two of a kind, I'd say."

Two of a kind? Eunice looked up. Mary Louise and she were the only ones left.

"By the way, Mary Louise, here's that book you were asking for the other day. It's no wonder you couldn't find it. Someone had *hidden* it." Mrs. Rindfuss gave Eunice a sharp glance. She handed *Intergalactic Mutiny* to Mary Louise and went back to her desk.

Eunice sat very still and stared at Mary Louise. Mary Louise was looking down, slowly picking up her books.

"*You're* Cosmic Cousin!" Eunice said at last.

Oh, no! It just couldn't be. She raced quickly through everything she knew about Mary Louise. Of course, Mary Louise did go to her school and she did study at the library, but Eunice had never considered her. She had thought that Cosmic Cousin would be someone more . . . exciting. Someone like Janie Hines.

Now that she knew, she almost wished she could go back to not knowing.

Mary Louise still didn't look up but she said in a low voice, "I found your note—about not leaving any more books under the table."

"But you're not wearing anything red," Eunice protested. There had to be some mistake. She didn't want it to be *Mary Louise Butterman*.

Then Mary Louise pulled up her sleeve so Eunice could see her watch. The band was bright red, all the numbers were in red, and there was a ladybug in the center. "It's not very big but I don't have anything else that's red," she said, looking down at her feet. "I

was going to show you my watch at school today. . . ."

"That means you already knew I was Solar Soulmate," Eunice said accusingly.

"Yes. I knew when you gave your book report on *Terrors of the Time Warp*. That was one of the first books I left a note in."

"What book did you do your report on?" Eunice asked.

"*Trapped in the Asteroid Belt.*"

"But I never heard it," Eunice said. And then she remembered. She had been home with the flu the day Mary Louise gave her book report.

Eunice thought of something else. "Why weren't those notes in your handwriting?"

"Oh, I've been practicing a new way lately. I like the way Eddie writes. Have you ever noticed his handwriting?"

Eunice nodded grimly.

"I think it looks nice. Sort of elegant," Mary Louise added.

They were silent for a moment.

"Why did you start leaving those notes in the first place?" Eunice asked.

"I got the idea from the *Pioneer 10,*" Mary Louise said.

"What's that?"

"It's a spacecraft they sent into outer space with a message from Earth. Maybe somebody in another solar system—way on the other side of the universe—will find the message. I like that idea. It's sort of like sending a note in a bottle." Now Mary Louise was looking right at her as she talked. Eunice had never heard her say so much. "My friend Sonia told me about it. She's always reading about science and space."

Eunice felt a twinge of jealousy. "You're lucky . . . having a friend like that."

Mary Louise looked a little sad. "She was my best friend before we moved. I guess that's why I started leaving the notes. I wanted to find someone who likes the things I do."

"Then *why* didn't you tell me who you were?" Eunice burst out.

"I thought if I kept it a secret, we could be friends—sort of. I wasn't sure you would want to know it was me," Mary Louise said.

Eunice winced at that. It was too near the truth.

"Girls!" The lights flashed off and on.

Eunice and Mary Louise grabbed their books and walked to the desk. Mrs. Rindfuss was waiting for them, tapping her foot. "Here it is, after closing time," she grumbled as she checked out Mary Louise's books. "It would have to be you two. How many times do I have to remind you of the library rule: Books must be brought to the desk fifteen minutes before closing time."

After Mrs. Rindfuss had shooed them through the door, they lingered on the steps for a few minutes.

"I should have left earlier," Mary Louise said. "I wanted to finish my Halloween costume tonight."

Eunice remembered what Marcie had said. "Your fairy princess costume?"

Mary Louise looked surprised. "Fairy princess? No. My comet costume. I have to glue more sequins on the tail part."

"A comet! Wow!" Now that seemed more like Cosmic Cousin.

"Could you help me finish my UFO costume?" Eunice asked.

"Sure."

Eunice was feeling happier by the minute. "Have you ever made a map of the constellations?" she asked.

"I started one last summer," Mary Louise answered.

They could hear Mrs. Rindfuss locking the front door. "Isn't it time for you girls to be going home?" she said as she passed them.

After she was gone, Eunice looked at Mary Louise and asked, "Who does she remind you of?"

"Mrs. Rindfuss?" Mary Louise thought for a moment. "The Martian Zyvitch?"

"Right." Eunice grinned. Only Cosmic Cousin would have known that.

About the Author

NANCY HAYASHI studied at the Cleveland Institute of Art and at the Otis Parsons School of Design in Los Angeles.

Although ashamed to admit it, she—like Cosmic Cousin and Solar Soulmate—used to hide her favorite books on the ledge under a table at her town library when she was growing up.

Ms. Hayashi now lives in Los Angeles with her family.